MOLLY: THE BEGINNING

ZOMBIE INSTINCT, BOOK 1

J.B. HAVENS

Molly: The Beginning

Zombie Instinct, Book 1

A NOTE FROM THE AUTHOR

This novella has been a long time coming. I've worked on it longer than I ever thought possible. Molly Everett is a special character, one who has been stuck in my head for almost two years now. Molly: The Beginning is just the start of what I hope will be a gripping series, one which will take you to the end of the world and back again. Thank you for taking a chance on her, and me, by reading this.

I'd also like to thank Brian Parker for believing in Molly. Thanks for your help, advice, and the answering endless messages and questions.

Sam, Kelle, Jules, and Jess, thanks for reading all the little snippets I send and being there for me. Zombies may not be your guys' normal genre but you've read it anyway. Thanks!

Casey Fry, thanks for being my friend and being even more excited for this book than I am.

To my mother and Aunt Linda. You've both been my cheering squad since I first decided to give this writing thing a try. Love you both.

Lastly, a special thanks to my husband and children. Thanks for putting up with my own unique brand of crazy and still loving me anyway.

CHAPTER 1

Red and black globs of rotting flesh slowly dripped off the length of my weapon, falling to the snow where seven corpses lay at my feet. The blood soaked wooden bat was slick beneath my palms, my fingers and knuckles ached from clutching it so tightly. My chest ached from exertion and my arms felt unnaturally heavy, twitching from the strain and stress I'd put them through. I was panting, my breath drying and cracking my lips in the frigid, winter air.

Another one was coming, shambling toward me, still four blocks away. Its gait was strange. *Missing an arm and having a broken ankle would do that to you.* Shoulders sagging, I looked down at my boots and the blood and gore staining them. I knew I was too exhausted to go another round with even just one more meat sack. Stepping over the bodies and attempting to ignore the squish of brains under my feet, I took a left out of the intersection and jogged as fast as my spent body could move. Stumbling and struggling for every step.

Burned-out cars lined both sides of the street, snow

covering them in a sticky film. The melting flakes mingled with soot and ash to make a stinking black mess. The world after zombies smelled like ash, blood, and rotting flesh. Some days I wondered if it would have been better to die quickly, back in the beginning.

Each step was slower than the last as I forced myself forward. The business district of the town I found myself in was just big enough to make a stop worth my while. Snow began to fall in earnest, cutting visibility down to less than twenty feet. I heard the slow, shuffling steps of the walking corpse following me. Soon, the noise would draw others. Forcing a burst of speed from my aching legs, I outdistanced it and took a left, out of its line of sight. Down an alley lined with overflowing dumpsters; even the cold was unable to temper the extreme smell of the rotting garbage.

I stumbled over something half buried in the snow, my boots slid and skidded wildly on the icy pavement of the alleyway. My shoulder slammed painfully into the brick wall of the building, stopping my helter-skelter slide. Heart hammering in my chest from the instinctual fear of falling, I caught a quick glimpse of what had fouled up my running escape.

Bones.

The ends were shiny from where the owner's joints had rubbed them smooth, reflecting grotesquely in the moonlight. A macabre freak show of death. Only this was no circus, this was real life. Where the blood congeals into a sticky, brown-black mess and screams half heard in your mind tell the all too familiar story.

I looked around frantically, desperate to find shelter. The cold seeped through my clothes and the wind began to howl and blow icy snow into my exposed face. A grocery store lay just ahead, not the best idea, but I was out of options. If the zombies didn't kill me, this weather would.

Hobbling now, I skidded past vehicles of all shapes and sizes in the parking lot. I'd tried a grocery store about a month ago and luck was the only thing that'd gotten me out of there alive. A band of survivors had taken up residency and were willing to defend their turf with screaming hot lead. Their poor marksmanship was all that saved me.

The front doors were intact and appeared locked. From experience, I knew the heavy glass was difficult to break and pointless to do so. If I made that much noise, I might as well just pop open the can of food and yell *dinner*! The storm was intensifying by the minute, I couldn't afford the time it would require to check the building out first. If anyone was in there, I'd have to deal with it then. First, I needed to get inside.

Past the overflowing dumpsters was a small loading dock and garage style, bay door. To the left of it was an emergency exit door. Slipping on the icy steps onto the dock, I was shocked to find a door with no knob.

"Of course, it's for emergencies only, they have bars on the inside, not knobs."

"Dammit!" I bitched aloud to myself and moved back to the bay door. Gripping the frigid handle, I squatted and lifted. My aching back and arms screamed with pain, but my efforts were rewarded—the door opened with a crack of breaking ice and a squeal of metal. It was loud and even though I wasn't sure how far the sound would carry in the storm, I only opened it far enough to slide underneath. Shoving my pack in first, I peeked under and saw darkness. I could be walking directly into a trap. My imagination ran away with me, conjuring images of dead fingers grasping at my hair and teeth tearing my exposed and vulnerable throat open.

"Nothing to do for it, just get in," I muttered under my breath. Laying on my back I slid inside, being sure to keep my bat ready. I'd pounded ten-inch nails through the end of it at opposite angles. It was messy, but got the job done.

The room was pitch black around me. My breaths echoed back to me with each gasping drag of air I forced through my lungs. I quickly slid the door shut behind me and grabbed my flashlight from my pack by feel. The narrow beam did little to illuminate the large room. Shining the light onto the bottom of the door, I found the bolts I knew had to be there. Sliding them into place, I secured the door behind me before continuing ahead. It wouldn't hold for too long, but breaking it open would be loud as fuck.

Metal shelves full of cases of canned goods and stacked boxes were everywhere. It was controlled chaos. I couldn't believe this place hadn't been raided yet; there was a huge stock of food in here.

"Security first, comfort later." *I really need to stop talking to myself...*

I followed the narrow hallway past a walk-in cooler toward double doors leading out into the store itself. I crouched down, hidden behind the black swinging doors. The howling of the wind outside was loud enough to cover any sounds from inside. I could hear the metal beams of the roof creaking and swaying under the force of the storm. Clicking off my flashlight, I gave my eyes a few moments to adjust. There was light coming from inside the store, not enough to see by back here, but enough to shine under the stockroom door.

Carefully pushing the door open, I crept out on silent feet. I found myself in the produce aisle, bombarded with the thick stench of rotting vegetables. Blue and black mold grew over each pile of food. I put the back of my relatively clean sleeve against my mouth and nose, though it did little to mask the smell. I could see now that the yellow light was flickering and shifting long shadows on the ceiling above it.

Candles.

I passed aisle after aisle, each one well stocked with enough supplies to last for years. Beside me were the long, white meat cases, where I'd expected to find putrid meat rotting in its own blood. Instead, they were empty and clean. I double-checked that the straps of my pack were tight and I held my bat in front of me with both hands. Inhaling deeply, I peeked around the corner of the shelf. I lowered my weapon when I saw that a small girl, not much more than sixteen, was huddled in a pile of ragged blankets. Candles lined the shelves near her, their empty packaging strewn around her. Dirty, unkempt red hair covered her face, and she hugged herself tight with pale skinny arms.

Ignoring her for the moment, I kept walking down the main aisle, checking down each row of shelves, straining my ears for any sound. I didn't think the girl would be sleeping if there were any zombies in here, but I had to make sure someone else wasn't going to try and brain me. People are more dangerous than the dead ones—at least they are predictable.

What the fuck do I do now? I thought. I couldn't kill her, but I also didn't want to wake her up and scare her into attacking. I spotted a few more blankets neatly folded off to the side. Carefully setting aside my pack, I propped my bat against the shelf and grabbed a handful of blankets. Spreading them out into a pile, I sat down. The simple act of sitting when I'd been on my feet since dawn was such a relief it was all I could do not to sigh aloud. You know you're tired when even cold tile floors are looking good. *Next time, I need to break into a mattress store.*

Using my pack as a pillow I laid back and tucked the remaining blanket over my shoulders. As comfortable as I figured I'd get, I shut my eyes.

CHAPTER 2

The storm battered the store for what felt like hours. The candles hissed and a few burned down until they put themselves out. I could hear the girl's rhythmic breathing as she slept. She cried out and mumbled in her sleep. Glancing over at her, I saw she was tangled in the blankets, thrashing against them in her nightmare. Limbs flailing, she screamed and I jumped into action. She had to shut up or they would hear her. Being eaten alive was not on my do-to list for the day.

Catching her thin wrists, I shook her awake. Blue-grey eyes met mine, imagined fear was replaced by genuine panic.

"Get off me! Who are you?" she screeched, loud enough to hurt my ears.

"Shut the fuck up!" I shook her sharply. "I'm not going to hurt you unless you don't stop that fucking screaming. I can help you, but not if you bring deaders down on our heads."

The shrill wails stopped abruptly. Her chest rose and

fell rapidly as she panted. "Let me go, please." Her voice was small and scared, showing the child she still was.

"If I let you go, you can't attack me with that knife you have under your pillow." Her eyes flicked to the weapon in question, the blade dislodged from its hiding place in our struggle. "Seriously, I'm not going to hurt you. Just relax." I loosened my grip on her wrists as I spoke. "I'm going back over there where I was. Just chill."

I kept my hands where she could see them and backed up slowly. Settling back on my makeshift bed, I gathered my knees up to my chest and rested my arms on them. "What's your name?"

"K-Kelle. I'm Kelle," she stuttered, but appeared to be calming.

"Hi, Kelle. I'm Molly Everett."

CHAPTER 3

"How did you get in here?" Her voice had lost its trembling. The strength I knew she had to possess was beginning to show. You couldn't survive in this world without it.

"The bay door was open." Seeing her panic, I hurried to reassure her. "It's locked now."

I didn't see either of us sleeping for a while so I helped myself to two cans of food from the shelf behind me. Blindly searching my pack, I found the can opener easily and was greeted by the syrupy sweetness of baked beans. "How long have you been here?" I mumbled around a mouthful of the beans. They were gross as fuck when cold, but high in protein and sugar.

"I'm not sure... a while. What do you want?" Anger was overriding her fear. *Good girl.*

"Some food and a place to wait out the storm. I'm beyond exhausted." Scraping the bottom of one can, I switched to the second. *Green beans, sweet. All I need is some fruit and I could pretend it was Thanksgiving.*

"What else?" She'd pulled the knife from under her

pillow and was twirling it around. It was a wicked looking Bowie knife, gleaming steel and razor edged sharpness. *I wonder if she knows how to use it?*

"Nothing," I shrugged.

"Nothing comes free or easy anymore. I may be young, but I'm not stupid. I haven't met any survivors that didn't want to either steal from me or rape me. Or worse." Pointing the blade at me, she patiently waited for my answer. Gone was the girl scared of her nightmare, in her place was a survivor.

"I don't have the necessary equipment to rape you, even if I wanted to. Which I don't. Like I said, kid, I need some food and a few days' rest. Nothing else. You don't even have to talk or look at me. I'll go into my own aisle."

"I could charge you for the food. I was here first. Finders keepers and all that."

Savoring the flavor of the last of the green beans, I didn't bother to answer her. Instead, I simply set the can to the shelf behind me, stowed my opener, and grabbed a couple bottles of water from the nearby case.

"Answer me," she growled like a dog defending its yard.

"No." I turned to the side, gathering my pack and dismissing her. "I already did. Go to sleep or whatever. I'm finding my own place to crash on the other side of the store. Keep your nightmares to yourself, kid. I'm not here to babysit."

Gathering my pile of blankets and gear to my chest, I went two aisles over. Picking the far end, I set up camp of sorts. As I did, thoughts of the first days after the infection and how it began to spread invaded my mind, back when the zombies first appeared. When the slow, trembling death of the world as we knew it began.

No one was quite sure how it started, just that it came from Africa and spread across the globe in less than a week. In six days, the news reported infections on every continent. By day eight, Europe was dark and silent. The last news broadcasts from the BBC warned people to lock themselves inside their homes and prepare to defend it and their families. The infected were dying, but they weren't staying dead. They rose and fed.

Next came scattered reports from New York, Boston, LA, Houston— every major city in the United States. The National Guard was overwhelmed and the police were overrun. Run, they said. Run and hide. There was no stopping the hordes of infected.

The few remaining radio stations broadcast lore from ancient times and pointed to evidence of the creatures' existence in most cultures across the globe. They were called 'draugrs' in Norse mythology, 'zombies' from Haitian lore and American pop culture, and the Greeks called them 'revenants'. There was no mention of how to prevent infection, how to stop the plague from spreading, or how to kill them.

Churches, mosques, and buildings dedicated to every religion filled to capacity with those ready to meet their maker. The End of Days had arrived in all its vicious glory. No majestically deadly horseman led the rampage, just scores of the infected. Mothers ate their children, husbands feasted on their wives, and so on, until the streets ran with blood and screams filled the air. The infected faithful died and rose, feeding on their own congregations. I watched the television screen in horror as the National Guard, trying to eradicate as many zombies as possible, razed churches. I kept watching as the stumbling, burning dead broke out of the barricades and fed even as they burned. Their screams played in my mind sometimes, over and over like a broken record of pain and terror. I couldn't decide which was worse, burning alive or becoming a meal for one of those damn things.

The last scientist I'd seen on CNN said that the infection rate was over ninety percent. If you were going to catch the disease, you would have by now. The few survivors left were naturally immune to the initial outbreak, but the virus quickly mutated, as viruses tend to do. Ensuring its survival, those who died from the original disease were able to transmit it through exchanges of fluid, like bites.

I sat in my tiny studio apartment watching until the television turned to nothing but static. The buzzing noise barely covered the near constant gunfire and screams outside. My drapes were shut and the lights stayed off. I was frozen in place and consumed by absolute terror.

Like most people, I only had about a week's worth of food in my home. Even by cutting my food intake by half I couldn't make it last. The power stayed on for a while, until finally, everything went dark.

Parting the drapes, I stared downward, watching and learning. Dawn was just beginning to lighten the night sky, a pack of zombies or whatever you wanted to call them, scrambled for shelter in a nearby store. One stood out from the rest, seemingly leading them. Their tattered bloody clothing exposing skin the color of ash. Many were mortally wounded, but still up and moving. The main pack was about eight strong, moving down the street in a horrifyingly organized manner. A few stragglers brought up the rear, stumbling and falling; they tripped often and ran into cars. Those at the rear of the pack were caught in the light. They didn't burst into flames like some B-movie vampire, but they howled in pain. Stumbling and trying to move faster, they finally made it to shelter.

"Fuck, this is bad." Waiting for the sun to rise completely, I

packed the little remaining supplies I had and left my home behind.

I pulled myself back to the present with a shake of my head. No good could come of thinking about this now. The only things left were surviving, one day at a time. Food, shelter, and now, heat. Basic necessities. People used to panic if their social media accounts were down for more than a few minutes or when their smart phone batteries died. Gone were the lattes, smart cars, and political correctness. Those that couldn't adapt died.

Natural Selection again ruled the earth and Man was no longer the top predator.

Like a giant clock, the death toll had chimed and reset. Some believed God was punishing us for our sins, others believed a New World Order had set it all in motion in order to rise to power. I didn't know what I thought anymore. Nature wins out, every time. Whether it was a comet or a virus, we were just blips in the grand cosmic plan, no more than a smudge on the screen—easily wiped away.

CHAPTER 4

I woke to an aching back and a full bladder. A weak, cold sun had risen, doing its best to shine inside. However, the grimy, boarded over windows kept the store shrouded in near darkness. Pushing myself up to stand, my joints popped and creaked. My body was battered and worn out. I'd been on the run in the wild for months now and never stopped or rested for longer than a day or two.

"Fuck this, I can stop here for a bit," I said, yawning before guzzling an entire bottle of water.

"Ya know, lady, talking to yourself is a sign of ill mental health."

I'd forgotten about Kelle. Coffee was sorely missed. "Some say it's a sign of intelligence. You'll just have to choose which to believe. I need to pee, you have facilities in here?" I was not looking forward to going to outside to piss, no fucking way was I hanging my ass out in this weather.

"Yeah... in the back. It still flushes, just fill the tank with water when you're done."

Sweet. Flush toilet, food, and toilet paper. *What more could a girl ask for? Oh yeah, coffee.*

KELLE WIPED her hands after breakfast. The baby wipes came in handy after meals, but every two or three days she braved a cold bucket shower over a floor drain in the back. The advantage of being stuck in here was you had everything you needed to survive. Soap, shampoo, and a bucket of water wasn't a steam shower, but it was better than sitting around smelling yourself or getting an infection. She followed up the wipes with a quick squirt from a bottle of hand sanitizer.

She didn't know what to think about that lady yet. She wouldn't go so far as to trust her, but if the woman wanted to hurt her, she would have by now. Maybe she was telling the truth and really did just need to rest for a few days. There was more than enough food here for both of them.

Was she really considering letting her stay? Asking her to? She didn't need help, she'd been on her own for months now, but having someone else around wouldn't be so bad. The lady, Molly she'd said her name was, might be good to have in case the dead came. It would be next to impossible to defend this place on her own. Her mind drifted to her family, the pain of their deaths still a fresh wound. She tried not to think about them too much. Her entire world consisted of surviving the day and not freezing to death. There wasn't much room left for mourning the dead.

"Kid!" Jerking toward the voice, she realized she'd spaced out for a bit.

"What?" Kelle snapped.

"Are you okay?" Concern crossed the older woman's features. Her short black hair was now wet and slicked back from her face. The blood spatters that decorated the woman's body last night were also gone, replaced by a new shirt.

"It's the apocalypse and I'm all alone; everyone I know is either dead or one of those things. What do *you* fucking think?"

"Look, I realize life sucks right now and it's even worse for you because you're full of teenage angst and shit, but keep a civil fucking tongue or I'll give you a lesson in manners."

"But you're allowed to cuss at me? That's hardly fair." Crossing her arms over her chest, Kelle tried to pretend she wasn't enjoying the parental-like attention.

"Cussing is fine, fuck if I care. Miss Manners isn't exactly going to jump out of the woodwork and cry about the misguided youth of the nation. But, can the fucking attitude, girly."

"Why should I show you respect? You broke in here in the middle of the night and stole my food. It's me who should be pissed at you." Standing and pulling her knife, she faced the older woman. She may be a kid, but she'd survived this long and not all of it by hiding. She'd done terrible things, just like everyone else has had to. Not wanting to think about that now, or ever again, she shoved those thoughts away in a box she'd created in her head.

With a rush of motion, Molly slapped her hand, knocking the knife loose and had her arm twisted behind her in seconds. The shelf scraped her cheek where Molly smashed her face against it.

"Let me go, you psycho bitch!" Jerking against the

hold, she earned nothing but a smack to her head. Jolting her face against the sharp metal edge once more.

"What did I fucking tell you, kid?" Grabbing her other arm, Molly pushed her head down and forward. Now both her arms were painfully pulled up behind her back, forcing her to bend over and hang her head. Burning pain in her shoulders kept her from struggling or standing up. "You may think you know something about defending yourself, but let me tell you—" Jerking harder, Kelle hated the scream that was forced from her mouth. "You know exactly dick. Next time you pull a knife on someone, use it. Maybe it makes you feel tough or look cool, but the longer you stand still with your blade, the better chance your opponent has to take it away from you."

The woman released her arms and pushed hard against her back, sending her stumbling forward. Hot humiliation burned her face and tightened her hands into fists. "Fuck you." Spinning quickly before Molly had a chance to react, she punched the woman in the face. Twisting her upper body into the motion, she utilized every ounce of momentum she could. Her knuckles split open on the woman's teeth, the *crack* of her fist striking flesh was overly loud in the otherwise quiet store.

Staggering, but not falling, Molly staggered backward. Turning her head, she spit blood in an arch. "Better. Much better. Maybe there's hope for you yet, kid." Smiling with bloodstained teeth, the older woman walked away.

"Well, fuck! Great, now I'm talking to myself too." Muttering, Kelle shook out her hand as the pain lessened by degrees. Blood seeped from her knuckles, coating her hand in a fine, red film. Hating the sight and the surging memories it evoked, she grabbed more wipes. Desperate to clean the stain away.

"I'm so sick of blood," she whispered to herself.

CHAPTER 5

I rinsed my mouth with water, spitting until the pink disappeared. Checking for loose teeth and finding a few, I was surprised at the girl's gall and strength, though I shouldn't have been. She'd been alone for some time; that much was obvious. This world was not for the weak, not anymore.

I used what daylight filtered through the covered windows to assess the security of the store. It wouldn't be a terrible idea to hole up here for a while. Surviving on the road was horrible enough, but in winter it was detriment to a long drawn out suicide. We'd have to solve the problem of how to heat the building because winter was here to stay. I could only hope that the cold would have an effect on the zombies. They wouldn't die of exposure, but if their bodies froze, they wouldn't be able to move. Or so I hoped.

Heading back out into the store, I found Kelle scrubbing at her hands like frigging Lady Macbeth. "Kid," I said.

She didn't stop, just kept on pulling more wipes out of

the container. A growing mound of baby wipes already at her feet. "Kelle." Stepping forward, I gripped her hands, halting her movements. "It's going to be okay." Her palms and fingers were bright pink from the thorough cleaning she'd just given them.

"How can you say that?" Her face was twisted with grief and coated with unacknowledged tears.

"Because, you have to believe it. Even if it's a lie." Sighing heavily, I released her hands, confident that she wasn't about to spaz further. "Life sucks. It always has. That hasn't changed. We have a chance here, a chance to survive in more comfort than most people will see again in their lives."

"We're just delaying the inevitable. Those things will get in here and they'll eat us. They'll gorge on our bodies until nothing's left—if we're lucky. Maybe we'll just be bitten and we'll get away. But that would be so much worse. Spending who knows how long, wandering the earth, forever hungry." She shuddered and closed her eyes. No doubt remembering people she'd lost.

"Do you want to give up? Just end it all now?" I asked. "That's your choice, but for me a chance at life is better than none at all." Grabbing my flashlight, I headed to the back. "Come on, kid, we have work to do. It's cold in here and I don't want to freeze to death, surrounded by food." I exhaled white clouds with every breath. Hypothermia was a bigger threat than the undead right now.

"Do you have a plan? Because a fire will give off smoke and draw those things in." Trudging behind me, she was literally dragging her feet but she *was* following. I'd take it as a win.

"First things first, we have to make a smaller area to heat. We'll empty shelves and move them or something."

Passing the meat cases, it occurred to me that I hadn't asked her who'd cleaned them. "By the way, who cleaned out the meat cases?"

Kelle tripped and stopped in her tracks. "M-my parents, me, a-and my little brother." Huddled in on herself, she followed me blindly.

Pushing open the stock-room doors with a bump, I saw the cooler again. "Oh, this might work." Grasping the long silver handle, I gave it a yank.

"*No!*" Kelle screamed long and loud. Horror unlike anything I'd ever heard came from her mouth.

The smell hit me first. A gust of warm air, heavy with the sweet-fetid stench of rotting flesh slapped me in the face. I had stepped into a horror movie. Time slowed to a minuet crawl. I felt every muscle in my neck working as I turned my head.

Stumbling toward me—too close to avoid, were three zombies. The first two were a woman, with ratty brown hair and a bloody mouth, and a man with a paunch gut hanging over his belt; a gaping bite wound on his face showed where he'd been bitten. Last came a little boy, death forever preserving his six-year-old face. Their ashen skin stretched too tightly on their bones. Starvation finds us all.

My ears rang as the man latched his fingers onto my throat, his dirty broken nails scratching my neck. I fell backwards, helpless to defend myself. Shock and fear froze me, giving me no time to react. Unarmed, I had little defense had I even been able to muster one. His teeth were sharp and pain ripped through my body even as my blood filled his mouth.

Kelle's terrified, agony-filled screams echoed through the back room. My fingers were numb, I couldn't lift my arms. The man bit through my collarbone and I screamed until I thought my throat would tear itself apart. The snapping of my bone lost under the volume of my pain. He shook his head back and forth like the animal he was.

The man grunted and moaned in pleasure as my vision went dark. My chest ached and burned—a cracking sound reached my now near-deaf ears. I managed to turn my head towards her, desperate to reach out to her, but was rendered helpless.

Kelle wasn't screaming anymore. Her mother and little brother had their faces buried in her stomach. Blood and bile poured from her body in a near wave. Their hands were inside her, pulling out organs to be sucked on and slurped down. Smacking their lips with every messy bite.

My body jerked, something lifted me upward only to smash me back down again. Glancing down, I saw that his hands were buried wrist deep inside my chest. The shiny white ends of my ribs poked up where my breasts used to be. *Was that my heart?*

Darkness swallowed me—my pain disappeared. With a shuddering breath, I closed my eyes.

CHAPTER 6

Watching from the screen before him, Dr. Sam Henderson was fascinated at what he saw. Three zombies, a family by the looks of it, were feasting on two women. One, a girl not yet out of her teenage years, the other was maybe in her mid-twenties or early thirties. It was hard to guess from the slightly grainy black and white image. The CCTV cameras in the small grocery store were easily hacked. He had his tech crew cycling through as many as they could trying to keep an eye on things in the outside world.

Buried here in this steel and concrete bunker laboratory didn't offer much in the way of current events.

"Where is this?" Sam asked the technician.

"About twenty miles from here, sir."

The scene playing out before him sent chills racing down his spine. The zombies left without finishing their meal. Normally they will strip their victims down to bone. Why had they stopped? Moving together, the family backed up and stood near the door as if they were guarding the bodies. His mind sped through all the known possibilities. Could it be?

"Send an extraction team, now. I want them in my lab within the hour. I need to see them turn and document it. Those two ladies are going to be something special, I can feel it." His palms began to sweat from his excitement. If these two became what he suspected; he'd have many years' worth of research to keep him occupied. Slicking his hair back with his palm, he did his best to contain his glee and remain professional.

❧

BURNING, monumental pain throughout my entire body jerked me into consciousness. My eyes popped open, then immediately slammed shut. A florescent light was above my head making me feel like my retinas were flaming out.

I tried to speak, but no words came. Even my scream was no more than a groan. I lifted my arms, only to be stopped short, they wouldn't raise more than a few inches off whatever I was laying on. Moving my feet produced the same results.

"Please try to remain calm, ma'am. You're safe. No harm will come to you here," a disembodied voice echoed throughout the room. Unidentifiable as either male or female, the electronic tones were more robotic than human.

"W-where?" I managed to force out.

"Where you are is of no consequence. Please be patient. I have informed my superiors that you're awake."

"Untie me!" I was terrified, the last thing I remember was having my heart ripped out. I could lift my head just enough to see my chest. I was dressed in a bra and shorts, the perfect unblemished ashen skin of my sternum shone dully under the bright lights. Panic unlike anything I'd ever known rose through my body. *Why is my skin that color?*

"My sensors show you have an elevated heart rate and body temperature. You need to remain calm, ma'am."

"Fuck you and your calm!" My voice was coming back quickly and my chest ached with my gasping breaths. *What's happening? Am I dead?* My ash-colored skin told me almost all I needed to know. I'd turned and oddly, healed. Zombies never healed. They were dead, shambling meat sacks of pus and rot. *What am I?*

My hyperventilating had finally taken its toll. My vision went spotty and dark. Gratefully, I passed out.

"She is astounding." Sinking his hands into his lab coat pockets, Dr. Sam Henderson observed the unconscious woman through the two-way glass. The scientist he spoke to simply nodded in agreement. Glancing over at his colleague, for he could not call him more than that, Sam suppressed his disappointment in his partner; something that had become a habit of late.

"You have nothing to say?" Even though he would no doubt disagree with whatever the halfwit managed to get past his vocal cords, any response was better than nothing.

"She doesn't react in the usual manner," the scientist finally managed to mutter in reply.

"There is nothing normal about her, Isaac. She heals for starters, and fear is overriding her hunger. Does she even need to feed?" he wondered aloud.

"There's one way to find out."

For once, Isaac Jessup said something worth hearing. "Good idea."

Leaving the observation room and purposely striding down the hallway to the storage room, he tried to mentally predict the probable outcome of this experiment. She would feed, that much was a certainty. None of the undead they'd captured, even the Alphas, had been able to resist fresh meat. There was something very different about this one. That she was an Alpha was absolute, but what kind? Reaching the store room, he pulled on the handle and shivered at the cold blast of air. Carts with prepared *meals* were lined up neatly, ready to be wheeled out and dispensed. Selecting one with raw beef hearts, steaks, and hamburger, he silently pushed it to her room.

The camera above the door tracked his movements and when he made eye contact, the magnetic locks disengaged with a loud click. Pushing the door inward with the cart, he left it close to her bed. She was still out and secured with thick nylon bands at her wrists, ankles, and lower abdomen. He was fascinated by the changes her body had undergone during her transformation. Her skin was the color of old ash, while her hair remained black as night. Her fingernails and lips were a pale blue. He'd personally witnessed the skin across her chest spread like a flower blooming. It was too slow to observe it move, but each blink showed more growth. Her heart had not been completely removed either, a piece remained like a seed that regenerated over time. He'd stood over her and watched the red muscle regrow and begin to beat. Her lungs had inflated and turned pink with fluid.

Unable to help himself, he reached out a single digit,

tracing the spot on her chest where the hole had been. Her skin wasn't warm exactly, but neither was it cold. Slightly chilled but a normal level of elasticity.

"So strange..." He trailed off, lost in thought of the possibility. Was this the next stage of evolution? Was she a super human?

"You know what's strange? Touching a woman who's tied to a fucking table."

Startled, he jerked his hand back, once again stuffing it into the pocket of his lab coat. "I see you're awake." He met her eyes, their grey irises ringed with red. Then, he noticed the pupils. They were large like a cat and he absently wondered if they would give her excellent night vision.

"Untie me," she snarled. Her fear was apparently gone and now replaced with rage.

Taking three large steps backward, well out of reach, he pointed to the cart. "I've brought you some food. When I leave the room, you'll be released."

"How about you release me now and I'll show you just what I think of you."

As fascinating as she was, being within striking distance of an Alpha zombie was enough to turn his bowels to water. "I think not. You'll feel better after you eat." Walking backward until he reached the door, he again make eye contact with the camera.

"I'm not hungry."

"What did you say?" It wasn't possible. She was a zombie, but even Alphas had to feed. There was no choice. Hunger drove them, it was their only need, overriding all other instincts.

"I said, I'm not hungry. Now let me go!" She pulled on her arms, lifting them a few inches. The brackets under her bed groaned from the stress she put on it. The straps dug deeply into her wrists, drawing blood that she didn't seem to notice.

"That's not possible..." He waved frantically at the camera, begging them to open the door. The loud click of the lock sounded and he rushed through the door just as a strap snapped with a loud *twang*.

He slammed the door shut behind him, his heart racing with fear and adrenaline. Looking through the small observation window in the door, he saw she was sitting up on the bed, both her arms free, pulling on the strap at her lap with both hands. It gave in seconds, the ends of the metal brackets clanging on the floor as she threw it aside. She freed her other foot even faster.

"Holy Mother of God." He gasped in utter amazement. She was a work of art, created by a virus and biology. *Why you? Why did you change this way and not the other?* Hurrying down the hall to his lab, he was anxious to run additional tests on her DNA. They'd collected several vials of blood when she first arrived but he knew he'd need new samples. Her transformation was not complete, not yet, he was sure of it. He just hoped he could unlock her secrets.

CHAPTER 7

My ears ached with the noise assaulting them. Even squinting, the light pierced through my sensitive eyes. I watched in amazement as the lacerations on my wrists from the straps healed. I wiped away the blood to find perfect skin, albeit ash in color.

"What's happening to me?" my voice trembled. I was terrified of myself. But angry, so incredibly angry. Rage unlike anything I'd ever known burned through my body. Steeling myself for the pain of the lights, I looked up and found the camera in the corner by the door. I'd seen the doctor wave at it before the door opened.

"The lights! Turn off the lights!" I waved my arms and pointed at the ballast on the ceiling. Moments later I breathed a sigh of relief when they blinked off.

Now that I was off the table and could see properly, I surveyed my surroundings. I was in a room about the size of an average hospital room with a standard bed in the center that looked to be bolted to the floor. The walls and floor were bright white; the only color in the room was the red meat sitting on a shiny stainless steel cart near the bed. Half of one wall was an observation mirror. If they thought I was fooled they had another thing coming. Giving the mirror the finger I wanted to figure out how to cover the camera and get that door open.

Touching the slick metal of the door I found it cool under my fingers, there was no knob, just a small window about six inches tall.

"Fuck." I did my best to ignore the smell coming from the meat behind me. The thought of that raw flesh should sicken me, but it smelled delicious and sweet. I'd lied to that doctor, I was hungry. I was so ravenous that I could feel my stomach twisting around searching for something to fill it. I refused to give in and eat people. That would make me no better than those things out there. Endlessly roaming.

"Please have a seat on the bed," the doctor's voice filled the room. There was a speaker in the ceiling next to the light, which would explain why I hadn't noticed it before.

"Why should I?" Taunting him was most likely not a good idea, but I was pissed off and it made me feel better. "Just let me go. I'm not going to hurt anyone." It sounded flat and desperate even to myself.

"I'm afraid I can't do that. You see, you are unique. In all these months since the outbreak we've never seen one like you. Not only do you speak and seem to retain your memories, you're self-aware. You know what you are and are understandably horrified by it. Your blood and body contains a wealth of knowledge that I cannot part with. You understand, don't you?"

"I understand that you've been locked in this bunker, or whatever this place is, safe from the horrors out there. You're a coward, hiding behind your walls and locks."

Resting my forehead on the door it took all my strength not to devour every scrap of flesh on that cart behind me. I wasn't an animal. *I am me. I am Molly Jeanne Everett. I won't give in.* The words became my mantra as I ignored the droning of the doctor's voice. I could hear my own heart, slowly beating. Nowhere near a normal rhythm, the thumps were sluggish, but strong nonetheless.

Standing against the door, I took stock of my body. The blue of my fingernails was strange, but oddly complimenting the grey tone of my skin, a naturally-occurring macabre manicure. The scar from when I cut my arm on the monkey bars in third grade was bright white, nearly electric in contrast to my now darker skin. *So, old scars remained but no new ones were formed.* Looking down at my chest, the space between my breasts was perfect and smooth. My fast healing was freaking me out. *What am I? How did this happen?* I'd seen dozens of people turn, not once did one of them heal anything or get more than a gurgling moan past their lips. Yet here I was, talking and thinking like I always had.

I'd seen Alphas before, so I had some concept of what this bastard was talking about. They led their hordes and seemed to have some basic communication but not speech. I had to get out of here. I knew how this went. First, they'd discover all they could from my blood. After that, they'd want to see just how much I could heal. I wasn't going to stick around for the torture portion of the show.

Pivoting on my bare heel, my eyes snapped to the cart of meat. Blood was slowly trickling off the side and dripping onto the white floor, each splat clearly audible to my sensitive ears. The red liquid was bright and grotesque against the otherwise clean floor. I couldn't ignore the smell any longer. The delicious aroma reminded me of that gut-clenching moment when I would drive past a fast food place and the wind blew the smell of french fries and grease into my car... Only this was more like starving, then being led into a buffet and told it's all you can eat. My stomach cramped with hunger unlike anything I'd ever felt.

My feet shuffled forward unwillingly. "It's not human. This is beef. No different than eating a steak. Granted... it's raw and bloody but it's not a person." Talking to myself did little to ease my disquiet at what I was about to do. The starving emptiness of my belly seemed to grow with every reluctant step. Inches from the cart now, the scent of meat was overpowering.

Reaching a trembling hand forward, I grabbed the closest piece of meat, it was cold and slippery. Using both hands I dug my fingers into the meat and brought it to my mouth. As soon as the flesh touched my tongue, my taste buds exploded with the flavor. Savory and delicious, I closed my eyes and tried to imagine I was eating steak tartar, which it sort of was, and not swallowing huge chunks of raw meat whole. Not bothering to chew beyond getting it small enough swallow, I quickly finished the steak. My brain clicked off and need took over. I shoved handfuls of meat into my mouth, moaning at the intense flavor. Cold blood trickled down my elbows, dripping on the floor. The hamburger was soft and didn't need much chewing.

Time sped up as my instincts took over, everything around me disappeared as I fed. For that is what this was. I was feeding for the first time and it felt amazing. My fingers slipped on the metal of the cart and my movements slowed. There was nothing left to eat. The cart was stained red, my fingers had made streaks in the blood like a fucked up modern art piece. I could almost see people in black standing around it with overpriced glasses of shitty wine, mumbling about its powerful message.

"How do you feel?" the doctor's voice filled the room once again.

"Full," I snapped. I started at my own reflection in the observation mirror. The white bra they'd put on me was now red. Evidence of my meal covered the lower half of my face and my arms were covered in what looked like red opera gloves. "I need a towel."

"Fascinating."

My ears buzzed and rang as my mind became clouded, my head feeling like it was full of cotton. "W-what?" I tried to speak, but it was no more than a whisper. Heat enveloped my body and sweat began to bead up and run down my skin, washing the blood away in rivulets. I could feel every muscle, each individual tendon and ligament. Holding my hands out in front of me, my vision blurred but I could see the muscles swelling. My forearms grew larger as I watched. Pain unlike anything I'd ever felt, even when being eaten, crackled through my limbs. My fingers seized and twisted into claws, my legs buckled and I smashed onto the floor. Losing control of my body, I curled into a ball, only to be jerked backward by the muscles in my back. Screams poured from my throat, high pitched and horror filled.

I was in agony and terrified that there was nothing I could do to halt the transformation.

This went on for what felt like hours but was only minutes. My limbs twitched and jerked as I continued to change. The fabric of my bra screeched as it ripped apart, followed quickly by the shorts. The seams unable to withstand the pressure of the expanding flesh they covered.

Slowly, as minutes ticked by, the pain melted away with every heartbeat. My body stopped seizing and gradually began to relax. Small spasms jerked my arms or legs randomly, sending shockwaves through my system. Finally, the pain trickled away as if it never was. I kept my eyes squeezed tightly shut, unwilling to see the monster that I'd become.

CHAPTER 8

Dr. Henderson watched open mouthed, staring in awe. "She's magnificent." His heart raced and sweat dotted his brow. Excitement thrummed through his body like a live wire.

"What just happened?" Isaac asked stupidly.

"History," Henderson answered. "She grew larger before our eyes. You can see her entire musculature defined under her skin. She went from emaciated to looking like a professional body builder in minutes. She'll need to feed again and soon. Send a nurse to clean her up and dress her. I want her restrained." Only rigid professionalism kept him from rubbing his hands together in glee.

"She broke them last time."

"I tire of you continuously stating the obvious. Unless you can contribute, keep your mouth closed." Losing his composure for a moment, Sam pressed the intercom, ordering a nurse to attend to his patient. "We cannot afford any mistakes. We may never again get an opportunity like this one."

"Understood," The nurse replied.

Scowling, Isaac left the room, perhaps shutting the door harder than necessary.

A short, heavyset nurse with long black hair carefully tied back swiped her keycard and entered the room, her arms full of clothing and towels. Molly remained on the floor, unmoving. Not even her chest moved as she breathed. The doctor was confident she was still alive—undead—he corrected himself.

The nurse's face drained of all color, fear tightening her features. Reaching out a hand, she gently touched her patient's shoulder. There was no response. Glancing over her shoulder at the mirror where she knew he watched, the nurse turned the woman onto her back.

Her nakedness bothered him. Her full breasts were stained with blood nearly the same color as her nipples. He thought it strange that her skin was grey but the subject's areolas remained pink and appeared unchanged in appearance from those of an uninfected woman. Uncomfortable and ashamed with his inappropriate response, Dr. Henderson turned his back to the mirror. He would give Nurse M, the only name her knew her as, a few moments to clean and dress his patient, and himself time to compose his feelings.

He counted to two hundred in his head before turning back to the mirror. What he saw confused him, he couldn't quite make out what he saw. The mirror was dark red, smeared unevenly across most of the surface. "What?" Getting close to the mirror, he squinted, just able to make out the remains of Nurse M. "Oh my god!"

The desk before him was equipped with a panic button. Smacking it, he braced himself for the screeching alarms and strobes.

A fist smashed through the glass, grabbing him by the throat. He gasped and choked, staring disbelieving at the grey arm holding him. The pressure increased, he could feel his throat collapsing under the crushing weight of her strength. He was jerked forward, his head and face smacking off the glass, once, twice. Dazed and out of oxygen he pounded on her arm, his blows weak and ineffective. The final thing he saw was his patient wiping away the blood on the glass. She smiled evilly before squeezing her fingers harder. Her face framed by red stained glass making her all the more terrifying. His bladder released in his final, shameful moment of life.

I DROPPED his dead and limp body onto the floor. His blood had sprayed like a fountain when I ripped his throat out. I moved quickly, wiping down haphazardly with towels and jerking the shirt and pants the nurse had brought onto my nude body. Grabbing her keycard, I wiped her blood off the plastic onto her jacket. I waved it at the door where a knob would be. A loud click sounded and the door swung open. Glancing left and then right, I saw no one. With no idea where to go to get out, I followed my ears. My hearing was excellent. I'd been able to hear the doctor's heartbeat behind the glass.

The alarm screamed and echoed through the long halls. I took a left, then a right, heading toward people. I'd make someone tell me the way out. Popping my head around a corner, there were troops ahead. Dressed in heavy riot gear and holding rifles, they no doubt blocked the exit.

"Hey, fuck faces, it's me, the killer zombie queen," I

shouted. "I won't hurt you if you step aside. Move and you can live."

Their gasps of shock weren't unexpected. A talking zombie? Who knew that was a thing?

"You know we can't do that," a gruff voice responded.

"I can kill all of you before you get a shot off. You willing to take that chance? I'm not the bad guy here. I just want to get out of this horror show. Move and live. Decide now." Leaning my back against the wall, I concentrated on hearing them. One voice, young by the tone, was all for letting me by. The commander said no, they had to stay put. I couldn't be allowed to leave. He threatened death to the cowards in his group.

Not giving them a chance to advance, I sprinted around the corner. My improved speed and immense strength took them by surprise. The first soldier I came to, I jerked his head to the side, and used his body to take the shot I heard leaving the barrel of the commander's weapon. Dropping the dead soldier, I swiped his rifle, firing into the remaining men. Their blood spread across the hallway like a river.

"Okay, so I was wrong, you did get a shot off," I quipped. "But I got more." Ignoring the alluring scent of their flesh, I ran further, keeping the rifle gripped in my hands. It felt strange and unfamiliar, as guns in general were a mystery to me.

Continuing to follow the sounds of panic, I skidded to a stop at what I saw through glass windows on either side of the hallway. Cages. Each housed zombies, six or seven to a room. They were regular meat sacks, not like me. These were the rotting, shambling corpses that I was used to. I slowed to a walk as I passed them. Each cage I came to, they stopped moving and stared at me. Their milky white eyes followed me, and they rushed to the glass, pounding on it. They screeched as they tried to reach me. The key card was still in my pocket, with a knowledge I couldn't explain, I knew they wouldn't hurt me. Swiping the card at each door I came to, the light flashed red. The doors wouldn't open.

"Fine, we'll do it the other way." Dropping the rifle, I picked a room. Tapping on the glass with my knuckles, it felt like plastic not glass. "Okay, Plexiglas. Let's see if this works." I backed up a step and eyed the spot I would aim for. Drawing back my arm, I punched the plastic. It gave with a crack and my arm was through to my elbow. Several mouths suctioned onto my skin, licking the blood off me. "Oh fuck, that's nasty. Stop it!" I shouted. They froze, not letting go of me but they stopped cleaning the blood off me. "Wow, okay, that's fucking weird. Let me go." One by one they released me. "Step back." Each zombie took a step back, like it was a game of Simon Says, only this was horrifying and not funny in the least.

Mentally filing the information away for later, I peeled the glass back, expanding the hole. I kicked to speed up the process and soon had a hole large enough for them to crawl through.

"Get out. Go feed," I ordered.

Scrambling out, they did as I commanded. Heading in every direction, the dead ones stumbled off, following their noses toward food. Guilt hit me momentarily, but I brushed it aside. If anyone deserved to die, it was the sick freaks in this facility. Not wanting to take the time to break any more rooms open, I ran down the hallway. I could smell fresh air now.

Following the hall, it twisted and turned randomly until I was turned around and unsure of my direction. My newfound powers kicked in and I followed my nose toward the fresh air I'd smelled earlier. At the end of the hall was a steel door, it looked the same as the one from my room. No knob, just a small window and a camera in the corner. I could hear screaming now, the zombies doing their job. Gunfire exploded in the distance. A battle raged, but in the opposite direction from where I was headed.

Waving the key card at the door, I was shocked when it opened. Maybe the nurse just didn't have clearance for the holding cells? Listening carefully before opening the door, I didn't hear anything. I swung it open flush against the wall. What I saw behind the door halted my forward momentum.

"Kelle?" I muttered.

The girl was drenched in blood and what I could see of her skin was grey like mine. All vestiges of the young girl I'd known were gone. She must have fed also, her muscles strained against the confines of her skin. Her eyes were the most disturbing addition, blazing red with no whites remaining. To say that they freaked me out was putting it mildly.

"This is your fault," she hissed. Her voice was strange, deep and crackly. Nothing like what I remembered from the store.

"I didn't do this. Let's leave here, together." Stepping carefully, I advanced toward her.

"Only one of us will be leaving," she replied.

She had a baton in her right hand and blood dripped off the end to land in thick splats on the tile. She grinned, exposing bloodstained teeth before letting loose a scream that could only be called a war cry. Then, she ran straight at me.

Her smaller body smashed into mine, knocking me

back against the wall. She brought the baton down, aiming for my face and head. Catching her arm, my arm shook with the effort of keeping her off me. It seemed that she'd inherited super strength also.

"Kelle. Stop." I gained some leverage and shoved her back through the doorway. I flung the huge door closed, trapping her on the other side. Screaming, she beat on the door, the impressions of her fists denting the metal.

"Fuck me." I turned and ran.

Hurrying through a series of more doors, the fresh air became stronger. "Almost out. Keep going." Arriving at a large, vault-like door with flashing red lights above it, I knew I'd found the exit. Spinning the handle, I heard the locks disengaging and clicking inside it.

Grunting, I pushed the heavy door open. Bright sunlight streamed in, stinging my eyes and forcing the tears to flow. I pushed the door shut behind me and turned the wheel until I heard the locks click back into place. I had to keep it from opening again. Kelle was still in there and would get free eventually. Not to mention the dozens of zombies inside. Grabbing the wheel with both hands, I pulled it down, breaking off the handle. Inside the wheel would spin, but with nothing to counter it, the locks would not release. Or at least, that was my hope.

Shading my face, I ran out into a field. I wasn't in a bunker under some city, I was right back in the middle of nowhere. There were trees as far as I could see in every direction. Snow crunched under my bare feet, but I felt no cold.

My skin was on fire, I had to get out of the sun. Now I knew why the undead rarely came out during the day. The light was painful to their sensitive eyes and skin. I didn't think it would kill me, but it was like being cooked slowly. Odd considering it was no doubt hovering near freezing temperatures right now. So much for my theory of the cold bothering the dead.

Sprinting for the trees, I was full of energy, feeling like I could run flat out for hours. Once I reached the shade of the forest, the feeling intensified. The oaks and maples around me held onto just enough of their leaves to offer some relief from the sun, weak though it was in the winter.

"Gotta find shelter, and then figure out what the fuck happened," I mumbled to myself. The sound of my own voice comforting in the otherwise silent forest.

My feet pounded through the snow and ice on the forest floor, I didn't bother to be quiet or hide myself. I was no longer afraid of the undead. It seemed I was, in fact, one of them. I would need to be careful of humans, however. They'd see me and try to kill me on sight. Rightfully so. I didn't think any of them would wait to let me explain that I was different and wouldn't eat them.

Thoughts flew through my head as I sprinted. They were a jumbled mess of questions that were impossible to answer. Why did this happen to me? How? There wasn't anything special about the zombie that had turned me, was the virus evolving? Obviously there were more Alphas like me, only I was stronger than they were. Kelle was changed, not herself at all. Whereas I felt more or less the same mentally. *As long as you disregard the desire to eat long pig—otherwise known as 'human'.*

Unable to reach any conclusions, I attempted to shut off my brain and just run. The sounds around me became my only thoughts. A deer in the distance, startled by me, bounded away with its white tail high in the air. The chittering of squirrels in the trees above, mingled with the sounds of birds swooping in the air and chirping. I felt every leaf beneath my bare feet, every twig that snapped and crunched. I should be in agony, with bloody, ripped feet and falling down in exhaustion. I could keep going for days if I wanted.

I let go of the questions and put as much distance between myself and that bunker as I could. There would no doubt be a back exit and I needed to be as far away as possible on the off chance that someone began to pursue me. I didn't know what I was or what sort of creature I was becoming. What I did know was that I would fight to the death before I allowed them to turn me into a science experiment.

CHAPTER 9

I don't know how many miles I'd travelled. I'd been running full out nearly all day. The sun was setting behind the trees in a blazing show of colors. Even the sunset seemed more beautiful to me now.

Another clearing opened up through the trees about four hundred yards ahead. Settled in the small open space was a farmhouse. The windows were boarded up and nothing moved. If it was occupied, I'd have a fight on my hands, but I needed supplies. Better clothes for one. The white scrubs I wore now would be a beacon in the dark.

Skirting the clearing, I circled the property, looking for any sign that people were living there. No tracks marred the perfect snow surrounding the building. There was nothing to indicate that anyone had been here in years. I just hoped that there would be something inside I could use. Sunglasses would be amazing.

Listening carefully, I crept slowly toward the house. I heard nothing but the normal sounds of the forest around me. The peeling white paint and cracked, sagging porch told its own story of neglect.

Carefully stepping up onto the steps, I hoped they would hold when they creaked ominously. "Well, if this isn't like every horror movie ever..." The thought gave me pause when I realized that I was the monster now, not the would-be heroine.

The rusty doorknob turned with a squeal and dust flew around in the air as I pushed the door open. Outdated and mostly broken furniture littered the room. Beer bottles, cigarette butts, and condom wrappers showed the house's purpose, long before the dead walked.

"Well, at least the kiddies used protection." Relaxing, I explored the house, finding much of the same in each room. Smashed bottles, graffiti, and evidence of parties.

Heading up the stairs, my bare feet left tracks in the dust. The first room I opened was the bathroom. Thankfully enough time had passed that the smell was gone but that did nothing for the sight of it.

I tried another door. Faded white lace and ruffles greeted me. "Sweet. Girl's room." Ignoring the bed and the leavings from a long ago party, I headed right for the closet. Popping open the doors, I found clothes of every color hanging neatly where their original owner had left them. They were mostly circa 1980 but it would have to do. Black jeans with a grey shirt and black jacket would work just fine. Stripping and changing, I found some shoes. Close enough to my size, maybe a little big but they would do until I found different ones.

A small vanity was tucked into a corner near the bed, pulling out the little stool, I sat. My reflection was blurry through the grime coating the mirror, a few swipes with my old shirt took care of that. The face looking back at me was that of a stranger. My eyes had huge pupils that were reflective like an animal. The grey iris's now rimmed with a red circle. Kelle's had been all red, with no other color left. What did that mean? My hair was much the same, but my skin...

Touching my cheek, I felt the softness that hadn't changed. It was the color that turned my stomach. To say that it was ashen didn't cover it. If I laid down naked in a spent fire pit, I would be completely camouflaged. My blue lips were left over from when I turned, same as the blue fingernails. I was me, but not me, at the same time.

"So fucking weird." No longer able to stand my reflection, I stripped off the top cover of the bed. "Do I need to sleep?" Dust flew into the air as I tossed the moth eaten blanket aside. The sheets underneath were crinkly with age and spotted with stains, but otherwise intact.

Barf

"Just ignore it. Pretend you're in a sleazy motel somewhere." I laid down and let my muscles relax into the mattress.

I didn't so much fall asleep as stop being awake. My eyes shut and a black void enveloped me.

CHAPTER 10

The house was run down and beat up. No doubt empty for years. He didn't like it, but with night-time here and heavy grey clouds threatening more snow he needed to take shelter where he could find it. Ethan St. Claire hurried up the stairs, the darkness concealing the tracks in the snow.

Opening the door, he crept inside quietly before softly shutting it behind him. Disregarding the mess of partying kids, he stalked through the lower level on silent feet. His only weapon was a Bowie knife which he kept out and ready for a downward strike. Glancing up the stairs, he saw bare footprints in the dust. Dreading what was to come, he tightened his grip and headed up the steps.

The threadbare carpet under his feet did little to muffle the thuds of his boots. Wincing at the noise, he reached the top landing and a long narrow hallway stretched out before him. Faded white curtains with large holes in the fabric covered a small window at the end of the hall, letting in an eerie glow from the reflection of the moonlight off the snow. Strange shadows twisted along the floor as the curtains fluttered in a draft.

Shrugging his broad shoulders to settle his pack more comfortably, he opened the first door on the left.

There was a figure on the bed.

SOMETHING WOKE ME, a noise or rustle of fabric maybe. Remaining perfectly still, I waited, hoping it was my imagination playing tricks on me. Keeping my eyes closed and holding my breath the click of the door opening was all the confirmation I needed. Someone was here. I could hear his heart beating and the scent of his body odor was distinctly that of a man.

He stepped closer to the bed and my time was up. The dark would hide my skin from a distance but not if he was right on top of me.

"Don't," I spoke, hoping it would throw him. Opening my eyes, I surveyed his features. Alarmingly tall, the man was dressed in a heavy jacket with the straps of a backpack over his shoulders. I didn't notice much else because the long knife held all my attention. "I'll go. You can have the house. No need for the knife."

Moving to sit up, I stopped short when he quickly moved forward. Sitting up put my face right in line with the small amount of light from the window. A shaft of weak light struck me directly in the eyes, making me blink and cringe in pain.

"The fuck?" His tone matching the shock on his face. "What are you?" Fear sharpened his voice and I knew he could see my grey skin and red eyes.

"Would you believe me if I said I didn't know? I swear,

I won't hurt you." I figured I could probably heal whatever wound he inflicted, but healing took energy and I would need to replenish it. I didn't want to be forced to feed on him. He was just a survivor, like me, trying to make his way in this fucked up world.

"You look like a zombie, but the dead don't speak. Tell me what you are!" Forgetting himself and shouting showed just how deep his fear and confusion went. Adjusting his stance, he towered over me, ready at any second to sink that huge blade deep into my head.

"I-I am a zombie." In a flash of movement, he had me by the throat. I could break his arm and feed it to him, but I didn't want to do that. "Listen. If I was going to eat you, don't you think I would've attacked when I heard you on the stairs? I could have jumped you and you'd be bleeding out on this shitty carpet."

"Why didn't you then? Huh?" he growled in my face, shaking me. "If you're one of them... I should kill you and keep you from making more like you."

"Then do it." I let my hands drop off his wrists onto the pillow.

The moonlight highlighted his profile for a moment. He was handsome and could have easily graced the cover of a fashion magazine. A lock of deep auburn hair fell over his forehead, covering his furrowed brow. Thick stubble covered his cheeks and even chapped, his lips were full and red.

"Well? What are you waiting for? Cut my throat or slam that big knife into my skull. I couldn't make this any easier if I was doing it for you."

His eyes met mine, they were the color of dark honey, thick and sweet. Fear overshadowed his other emotions, but hiding in the depths was curiosity.

"I'm going to let you go. If you try to attack me, you better make sure you do a good job of it because otherwise I'll kill you with my dying breath." Cautiously and ever so slowly, he slid his big palm off my throat. If I had to breathe like a normal person, I'd be gasping for air.

"Sorry to disappoint you, big guy, but you're not my type." I wasn't allowed a type anymore, being dead kind of emptied the dating pool.

"Do you have a name?" he asked, crossing his arms over his broad chest and staring me down. He was blatantly suspicious—which was pretty freaking understandable considering the circumstances.

His question took me by surprise. From near death to small talk in the space of a second. "Sure. Do you?" Sitting up, I swung my legs off the side of the bed.

"Ethan. I'm Ethan St. Claire."

"I'm Molly Everett, the talking zombie. Pleasure to make your acquaintance." Smiling as big as I could, I tried to be reassuring, but he looked pretty freaked out. I guess he was entitled; I would have been too, if the roles were reversed. "Chill. It's fine. I'm new to this too."

"This is so wrong on so many levels."

He rubbed his forehead with his free hand, no doubt feeling a headache coming on just from the strangeness of it all. Just when you think the apocalypse can't get much worse, the zombies start talking. "I couldn't agree more."

It felt better than it should to have a normal conversation, well, what passed for normal for me these days. Talking to a psychotic doctor and some weird robot sounding voice didn't count as conversation, and before that it was just Kelle, which was mostly yelling. "Here I thought I'd punched my ticket, and gone off to the great buffet. But then I woke up like this, just as confused as you are now."

"I need a minute," he said, giving me the classic 'talk to the hand' gesture as he left the room.

"Well, just because I'm dead doesn't mean you have to be rude!"

The slamming of the door was my answer.

CHAPTER 11

A *zombie? That talks?*

"What the fuck?" Pacing the hallway, Ethan tried to decide what to do. A glance out the window told him enough, he couldn't leave in this storm. The white crap was falling fast and thick, adding to the few inches that had already covered the ground.

He should be in there chopping her head off. But killing her was very different from killing zombies. They didn't talk. They just made their way through the world looking for their next meal. Killing that thing, Molly, would be too much like killing a person. Somehow, he'd managed to survive this long without killing people. Violence was an everyday necessity now, but that didn't mean that he was going to give up the last slice of his humanity.

With his decision made, he went back into the bedroom. He didn't speak to her while he pulled out a few candles from his pack and set them around the room before lighting them. The soft yellow flames flickered and danced in the drafty house. It was a risk, but not a huge one. The light wouldn't travel too far in the storm outside.

"Come into the light," he said. "I want a better idea of what I'm dealing with."

Using one greyish colored hand to block the light from her face, Molly squinted and dropped her hand. "Make it quick, the light hurts my eyes."

Black hair hung in waves to just past her chin. She was short, he decided, the top of her head didn't quite reach his shoulder, but her physique was surprising. Muscles rippled under her skin, easily seen through her clothing. It was disconcerting and more than a little strange. Body-builders worked half their lives and didn't look even a fraction as cut up as she did.

"How strong are you?" It was sheer, perverse curiosity that made him ask.

Shrugging, she looked around the room. The bed frame was an iron four poster. Grabbing the nearest corner with both hands, she braced her legs, and pulled the post down; neatly bending it in half. "Pretty much a girl version of Hulk over here."

"What are you?" he asked, repeating his earlier question. He knew he sounded like a broken record, but he couldn't help himself; he was dumbfounded. The evidence was literally staring him in the face. She was a talking, self-aware zombie. As if the apocalypse wasn't bad enough already...

I MADE myself remain as still as possible, knowing that his trust was weak, understandably of course. I decided to start at the beginning.

"I was running from a storm and beyond exhausted. I found a grocery store and broke in. There was a girl in there, Kelle. She was sixteen if she was a day." Standing, I walked over to the window and resisted the urge to pull back the curtains.

"I heard a noise in the walk-in cooler and opened the door. Turns out that Kelle had locked her family-turned-zombie in there. After I was bitten, turned, or whatever; I thought I was dead. Everything went black and still. Just empty. But then I woke up."

"Keep talking, I'm listening."

Arms crossed defensively over his chest, I didn't know how much of my story he believed, but I kept on. "When I came to, I was tied to a table and my body had healed. My heart had been ripped from my chest but I still turned. The doctor there told me that I was an Alpha. You've seen the zombies that seem to be leaders, right? I guess I'm one of those, only stronger. He was trying to figure out why I'm able to speak and heal."

"How did you escape?" He stayed on the other side of the room from me, well out of my reach, or so he thought. I could be on him and have my teeth in his neck in seconds. His heartbeat was loud in my ears, and I could smell the blood flowing beneath his skin. If I could sweat, I would have, just from the effort it took not to rip him apart. I felt like an alcoholic in need of a drink while standing at the back of an AA meeting. Force of will alone kept me from tasting the sweet, candy-like flesh of his neck.

I hesitated, knowing he wouldn't like to hear about me attacking and eating part of the nurse. I had done it out of desperation, not desire. "I attacked a nurse. Killed her and stole her security badge." I tried not to think about it, but it was impossible not to remember the warmth of her blood as it slid down my throat, the feel of her heartbeat under my teeth, pounding so fast and hard before slowing; fighting to stay alive until it no longer could. I'd ripped out her throat and pulled open her chest like a foil-wrapped packet of leftovers. I tore her apart with ease, desperate to get to the goodies inside. Shaking loose the memories and the temptations they brought, I took a small step back—keeping myself as far away from Ethan as possible.

He flinched, his hand at his waist, now resting on the handle of his knife. Keen senses honed from months of survival kicked in; he knew what I was thinking.

"Relax. As delicious as you smell, I'm not going to eat you."

"You know that you telling me I smell delicious doesn't endear me to you, right? Kind of makes killing you seem like a good idea."

"Yeah, good luck with that." Rolling my eyes, I continued my story. "They had cells full of the dead. A whole hallway full of rooms. When I walked past them, their eyes followed me. I could *hear* them, *feel* them inside my head. They grabbed my arm when I punched through the glass. I told them to stop, to get off me, and they listened." Shuddering at the memory, I continued, "I let them out, used them as a diversion and escaped." I decided not to mention Kelle; he looked plenty freaked out without me adding the child-zombie from Hell onto him too.

"I can figure the rest out," he said, pacing back and forth, and fiddling with the strap of his backpack. "Listen, my instinct is to kill you where you stand." I tensed, angling my body into the best position possible to attack.

"Calm down. I'm not going to. Looks to me like there's some reason that you're the way you are. It's not up to me to decide what that is. You were changed into this, no fault of your own. Have you considered how much good you could do?"

"What do you mean, exactly?"

"If I were to believe you, and I'm not saying I do. Say you can *hear* and command the zombies, could you, I don't know, order them off a cliff or something?"

His idea gave me pause. This was all so new and had happened so fast I hadn't thought about it. He was right, I could influence the dead. Maybe I could be the undead superhero? I needed a name and a catch phrase. As long as I didn't have to wear tights or have my tits hanging out everywhere while a pair of short-shorts rode up my ass, we were good.

KELLE LICKED HER FINGERS CLEAN, the blood sticky and sweet like red honey. "That was amazing, was it good for you?" She laughed, looking down at the body of a teenage boy. His insides were still warm enough to steam wetly in the frigid air. The snow around his body stained a red so bright it was nearly florescent. From his neck to groin he was empty, as if he'd been hollowed out with a giant spoon. "No spoon, just me," she sang in a singsong voice. "Just me—just me."

She continued to sing as she danced across the snow. Her tracks were red from the blood dripping off of her. Able to hear heartbeats, she was a destructive force that was able to gain entry into every survivor's house or camp she came upon. They trusted her because she could talk, attributing her blood soaked body and grey skin to being in the wild alone. A pretty young girl couldn't be a threat, right? How wrong they were. She took joy in decimating every group that she came across. In the day and night since she'd escaped the facility she'd managed to infiltrate and destroy three groups, nearly a dozen people. Behind her, like a Pied Piper of zombies, she led a growing horde. After eating her fill, she opened the doors of the barn where the boy had been a lookout, and basked in the screams that filled the air.

"It sure is good to be me." Throwing her arms wide in the falling flakes, Kelle danced and twirled. Full of energy and stolen life, she was joyous in her destruction. Soon screams filled the night, only to be cut short as throats were eaten, abdomens opened, and the warm entrails pulled free.

"Now to track that bitch, Molly, and make her pay for what she's done." Reaching mental fingers outward, she felt the dead around her. Their empty minds were commanded easily, no spark left in their craniums. Her feet remained rooted to the earth and she mentally stretched further and deeper into the forest, searching for a spark. Skipping over animals, startled by her prodding they fled into the trees. Over a hill and across a field, there —a house, and within it, the warmth of a human and the answering cold fire of Molly.

"Got ya." Kelle's eyes snapped open and her grin was as evil as they come. "One, two, three, ready or not, here I come!"

CHAPTER 12

I jerked as if shocked, putting a hand to my forehead. *The hell?* Shaking my head, hoping to lose the strange feeling, I caught Ethan staring at me again.

"Look, I know I'm somewhat of an oddity, but this ain't no freak show, dude." Crossing my arms over my chest, I cocked a hip to the side and glared at him.

"I can't help it, sorry," he said from the floor where he sat, his back against the wall as close to the door as he could be and still be in the room.

He pulled his pack closer and then rooted around inside before pulling out a granola bar and a bottle of water. It seemed like only hours ago that I remembered doing the same thing.

"So, back to the superhero theory. You think I should turn into some sort of undead killer queen?"

"Think about it," he said around a mouthful of food. "If you can boss them around, why not? Maybe you alone can't rid the world of our zombie problem but the more you kill, the less there are to eat the few people left."

"Where do you factor into it?"

Laughing, he took a drink of water, then recapped it and put it away. "Nowhere. Sorry lady, but I want to get as far away from you as possible. No offense."

I was slightly taken aback. Was I that bad? Oh yeah, talking zombie... so yes, I was. "Well, okay then. I'll just be on my way. After all, I'm dead. A little blizzard can't kill me, right?" Walking to the window I pulled back the curtain and saw that the storm seemed to have intensified, something I hadn't thought possible. Great. "Never mind. I can't see the ground. I fucking hate snow."

"Why do I feel guilty right now?"

Glancing at him over my shoulder, I raised an eyebrow in response. "That's between you and your conscience. Either way, I'm done with this conversation. It's getting close to self-recrimination, apologies, and life-stories. I don't do that. I found this room first, so if you could, ya know, go find your own, that'd be great." I smiled my best customer service smile and waited.

"Nah. I don't think so. Maybe I believe your story, maybe not, but either way I'm not letting you out of my sight while we're in the same building."

"I already said I wasn't going to eat you and I meant it." Even as I said it I understood his motivation. If I was in his place I'd have killed me by now.

"Be that as it may, I don't trust strangers. Even before the world went to shit. The apocalypse has drained what little trust I had." Standing, he shouldered his pack. "Did you check out the rest of the rooms?"

"No. Don't need to. I hear heartbeats, remember? And zombies don't bother me now." I thought about telling him about the bathroom but figured I'd let him find that surprise on his own.

I continued to stare out the window while he left to

look around. My mind went back to that strange sharp pain I'd had. It had disappeared as quickly as it had come. It felt similar to when I'd "talked" to the dead in the bunker, but this was more powerful. My thoughts automatically drifted to Kelle. Was she trying to track me? Fuck, I hoped not. The last thing I wanted was a zombie *battle royale* in the snow. Could we maybe reschedule for the spring? The more I thought about it though, the surer I was that it *was* her. It made sense to my gut in a way that was hard to explain.

I needed to make a plan. Maybe I needed to test my abilities and see how strong I really was. Running through the forest was one thing, fighting zombies was another. I shivered at the memory of the weird mental connection I had with them in the lab. It was like my head had been full of worms, all of them wriggling together at once.

Ethan came back into the room, moments later. "This is the only slightly habitable room." He cast a disgusted look at the trash and mess lying in piles. "Looks like we're stuck together for now."

"Take the bed." I turned back to the window and watched the snow continue to fall. "When the storm stops, I'll leave." I didn't tell him but I may not wait that long. I scared the crap out of him and that's the last thing I wanted. I felt enough like a freak just by myself, being around him and practically smelling his fear made it that much worse.

"How do I know you're not going to rip my throat out while I'm sleeping?"

"You don't. I give you my word that I'm not going to, but there's no practical reason for you to believe that." I shrugged. My emotions, what I had of them, were pin-balling around in my head. I didn't know what to think or feel. Everything was *more* now. The weight of every decision was heavier, fear had a taste, worry a thick smell that stuck in my nose and throat. I knew that I should at least attempt to be considerate of his fear of me, but my own self-horror overrode it.

"You're right, I don't believe you." His shoulders tensed and I could smell the change in him. Fear was a thick, sickly sweet smell, like stale sweat and honey. His hand went to the knife on his waist and I was on him before he even finished his thought.

Grabbing him by the throat I hoisted him up and against the wall. I kept the pressure just light enough that he could still breathe but there was no chance of him getting loose. His hands pawed at mine, nails clawing desperately.

"See how easy that was? With a flick of my wrist I could snap your fucking neck and take joy in the sound." I squeezed harder, his flesh felt as thin as paper under my immense strength. When his face turned purple and his eyes rolled back into his head, I released him. He fell to the floor like a sack of potatoes. Boneless and heavy. "But I won't. I told you, I'm not going to kill you. I get that I freak you out, but try walking in my shoes once, pal. I fucking terrify myself."

Faster than I thought possible for someone halfway to oblivion, he pulled his knife free and buried it hilt-deep in my calf. Screaming in rage, more than pain, I jerked the knife out of my leg. Black blood oozed from the wound, soaking my pants and sock.

"That was a mistake," I growled. Crouched over my wound, I stalked Ethan with my eyes as he rose above me on trembling legs.

Dropping the knife, I flew upward in an explosion of

speed. Using my considerable strength, I pinned him to the wall. His face was inches from mine, his mouth opening and closing soundlessly. A few bubbles of blood popped near the corners of his lips. My arm was elbow deep in his chest. I'd punched my fist straight through his body, I could feel his heart twitching against my forearm as it tried desperately to beat. The sharp ends of his broken ribs cut my arm. Ignoring the pain was effortless when a meal was so close at hand.

"P-ple-ease," he gasped, each breath a struggle. Ethan's failing body spasmed in pain. His eyes were glassy, staring into my own.

"You had your chance. This is your own fault." I gave in, even as my mind screamed at me to stop, I sank my teeth into his neck. His flesh was warm, blood hot, and salty. I ripped my hand free, letting his body fall heavily to the floor. I followed it down, sinking to my knees beside him. I let my mind shut off and my instincts take over. I tried not to notice how sweet he tasted or how amazing it felt to eat. The wound on my calf knit back together, stinging and burning as it did so.

I slowed and then finally stopped feeding. Full and stated, my body surged with power. Energized and alert, I felt like I could run for a year and not tire. Cocking my head to the side, I listened, not with my ears, but with my mind. Kelle was coming, I could feel her as an itchy tickle behind my eyes.

"It would be rude not to go out and meet my guest. Very rude indeed. Mother taught me better manners than that."

To Be Continued . . .

Molly: Immersion now available!

PREVIEW OF MOLLY: IMMERSION

The smell was overpowering. Thick and viscous, sweet and cloying; it clung to every inch of her skin and hair. Rotting flesh and congealed blood coated her body and those around her. Her following, her horde of dead, her *children*. It didn't matter that some were falling apart or missing limbs, she cared for them just the same. The stench was a part of them and therefore a part of her. They were hers and she was theirs. She could feel their minds, the spark that animated them. The virus inside all of them spoke to her. More than a radio signal and less than speech, it had no words and no images. It was just the tugging of a thousand strings pulling each of them to her. She was at the center of an intricate web.

Kelle stood among her horde, hiding in a barn. The newly risen sun shone through cracks in the old barn's walls. The daylight burned like fire, even the weak early light of the winter dawn was like a blowtorch to her eyes. A beam touched her bare arm, the grey skin instantly burning and itching from the touch of light.

"Move!" Shouting wasn't necessary, but some habits were hard to break. Quicker than speaking, the more she did it the easier it became. With her thoughts, she pictured in her mind what she wanted them to do. She needed a circle, with her in the middle so their bodies would block the light from touching her. The direct sunlight would affect them, but the care of her horde didn't extend that far. They were tools and while she appreciated their usefulness, they were still just tools that could be replaced.

That was one advantage of the lab: not an ounce of daylight to worry about. It was just cold steel and the dead —a high tech tomb. After Molly locked her inside, she took the time to explore and had freed the first of her horde from their cages. She'd found Molly's room also; saw the bodies, what was left of them anyway—smelled the blood.

She'd been in her cell, the sweet taste of her meal still lingering on her tongue when looking down she saw the skin of her arms beginning to ripple, heralding searing agony racing through her muscles. Screaming in fear and pain, she fell to the floor on her hands and knees. Her back arched and joints popped as her body transformed. Her clothes ripped and fell to the floor, her arms and legs now too big for the small garments. Her shoulders jerked forward, forcing another scream from her throat as the muscles and tendons shredded apart before rebuilding. Her legs collapsed under her and she fell flat on her face. No longer able to scream, she moaned as her body continued to spasm and twitch as it finished changing with pops and snaps. A black wave of exhaustion pulled her under, her eyes shut, and refused to reopen.

When she awoke, she was back on the table with new clothing.

"The hell?" she croaked, her throat raw and sore. Lifting a trembling hand, she wiped the back of it across her dry lips.

"Please try to remain calm. You've gone through a transformation and need to rest."

Her mind was fuzzy and disorientated. It seemed as if the room spun around her. Sitting up only made it worse, but after a moment she swung her heavy legs over the side of the bed.

"Let me out of here." She stared at the camera in the corner, the blinking light seeming to mock her distress. Anger tightened her grip on the edge of the table until her heard the metal groan. Glancing down, she saw near perfect imprints of her hands in the bed. She wondered just how strong she was after the change.

Standing slowly and letting the dizziness pass, she walked to the door and pressed her hands against the smooth metal surface. Making a fist, she punched the metal lightly and a dent appeared.

"Get back on the table. Now!" the voice above her commanded.

"Yeah, about that." She punched harder, the dent went deeper still. The small window in the top middle of the door broke easily. Cuts appeared in her flesh and then vanished just as quickly. Testing herself, she kept beating on the door harder until the metal screamed and bent inward. She stepped back a few feet and eyed the door. The hinges and latch were the weakest points. Aiming for the edge of the doorframe, she got a running start and used her body as a battering ram. The door bent further outward. She ran at it again, this time creating a gap in the frame that allowed her to see the hallway outside. Two more hits and the door broke off the hinges and hung sideways. Shoving it aside, she climbed over the remains of the door and into the hallway.

There was a guard there, standing immobile in shock. His

rifle hung useless from a strap on his chest. Catching a whiff of him, she smiled and lunged. He reacted too slowly for her incredible speed; his attempts to bring up his weapon were useless. Her arms snaked around his neck and her knees slammed into his chest, causing him to tumble backward. Kelle rode him to the floor, tearing into the man's throat on the way down. She ripped off his helmet, tossing it aside, and bit so deep into his neck that she gagged on the spurt of blood.

The flavor was amazing. His flesh tasted better than any meal she'd ever eaten as a human. His screams died quickly and she fed until she couldn't eat anymore. His body lay in pieces at her feet and she wore a dress of blood and gore.

The alarms wailed, the red and white flashing lights burning her eyes. Shielding her eyes, she looked at the floor and followed the hallway to the right where the smell of blood was coming from.

The blood trail she followed had cooled and was slippery under her bare feet. Every step added to the tracks already left by that bitch, Molly. Her mind felt strange, like it wasn't her own. There was an invader. She could feel it swimming through her body, changing things—the same way she'd changed after they'd wheeled a cart full of meat into her room. Her muscles rippled and stretched with every movement. Stepping over the remains of a nurse, Kelle looked through the fist-sized hole in the glass and discovered the twisted body of the doctor. He was the same one who'd spoken to her. Or tried to anyhow. Something was missing from inside her, she felt wrong, as if she was someone else. There was enough left of her own mind that she wanted to find out why. Seeing the ID badge clipped on the doctor's pocket, she knew it would get her out of here. The hole in the glass was too small to fit through, but that was dealt with easily.

Smashing it open with her fists only took a few minutes,

the cuts she received from the sharp edges healed in seconds, before she even had a chance to feel it. Climbing through the glass, she dropped down next to the doctor's corpse, landing in a crouch with terrifying feline grace.

"I'll take that." Grabbing the badge and patting his cheek, his cool skin was still soft and pliable under her touch. "You really screwed the pooch this time, didn't you, Doc?" Kelle chuckled to herself.

Stretching her arms over her head, she groaned with pleasure at the feel of the strength she now possessed. "I'm really starting to like this new me. Feels so good." She ran her hands down her body, smearing the blood all over her skin, enjoying the slickness of it along her body. It felt so amazing it was borderline erotic.

Skipping down the hallway, she found a line of cages full of zombies. They called out, reaching for her. Using the keycard she opened doors as she went, the zombies inside immediately followed her. She could feel them in her head, squirming around and bumping together. Commanding them came naturally, there was no learning curve. She thought it and they did it. Easy as pie.

A set of wide double doors ahead had a sign that read **'Authorized Personnel Only'**. *"Bingo, my friends." Talking to the dead horde behind her felt as natural as talking to herself. In a way it was the same. They shared a mind, her mind. She could feel that now. Every minute she was near them, the closer they became. "Stay here, my pets. This is for Mommy's eyes only."*

Tapping the key card on the scanner near the door, a loud metallic click sounded and she pushed the doors open with a flourish. Florescent lights turned on with the opening of the door. Shielding her eyes with one hand she slapped at the wall with the other until she found the switch, blessed darkness was a cool relief to her burning eyes. The smell was the first thing to greet her, not the sweet, ripe smell that accompanied a beating heart but a nasty rancid odor of chemicals and rotting meat.

"Well, well, well, Doc. You were a baadd boy." Gurneys with sheet-draped corpses were in a long neat row. A quick count revealed seven in total. "Let's see what's behind door number one!"

Flipping the sheet off the first table, Kelle found the body of a small boy, twelve or thirteen maybe. His left leg was missing from mid-thigh down, the wound ragged and torn. No doubt the cause of death. The doc had opened the chest cavity and removed all the organs. She didn't know a lot about anatomy but there should be something in there at least. Leaning closer she gagged at the sharp chemical smell that preserved his little body. His face looked strange, smushed and half formed, like someone pushed on the clay before it was dry. Kelle felt his face, squishing and shifting the skin around as if he was wearing a mask. Tracing her fingers into his hair she felt the incision then. Catching the edge, she pulled forward, the boy's face folded down and exposed what was left of his skull. The doctor had cut off the top of his skull and the brain was missing.

"Eww. Come on, dude. What the hell? Waste of perfectly good brains here!"

Each corpse she looked at was the same. Hollowed out chest and bellies, empty brain buckets. Only three remained. "One, two, three!" she sang, ripping the sheets off them one at a time.

"Hello, Mother. Hello, Father. Hello, Brother. Here I am...at camp..." Shrugging and giving up on the song, she stared at the empty bodies of her parents and brother. The doc brought them here from the store. Each had a neat bullet wound to the forehead. She knew she should feel something, anger or sadness maybe, but the emotions she did feel felt far away and fuzzy.

Like a radio that needed to be tuned, she could sort of hear the song, but it was distorted.

Leaving the bodies behind, she made her way over to a long bank of computers. In all the confusion, some idiot had left his on. Sitting down, she saw file after file, some with videos and some just reports. One of the videos showed the doctor and a few assistants slowly dissecting a live zombie, their monologue stating their purpose of discovering an alternative to brain trauma for killing them. They were unsuccessful.

*One video file caught her eye. It was labeled, '***Alphas Transformation***'. Clicking on it, she sat back to watch.*

The screen showed the back room of the grocery store, Molly opened the cooler and her undead family burst free and attacked. She relived it in her mind as she watched. She felt the sharpness of their teeth, the searing pain as her mother and brother tore her apart. She saw herself die.

"This is fucking weird as hell." Shuddering she moved to close the file, but what she saw on the screen froze her in place. Her family stopped feeding and stood. They put their backs to the door as if they were guarding their now dead victims. "Why did they stop?"

The doctor had made audio notes on the video file. His voice was loud in the otherwise silent room. Apparently sometimes the dead do speak.

"The behavior we see here is consistent with the other Alpha subjects we have observed in the field. The attacking zombies seem to sense their queen's transformation. They stop feeding before the point where the Alphas would be unable to turn. Often they guard the queen until the subject has risen and the transformation is complete. In the field, the attackers often bring food to their queens, no doubt to assist in completing the extreme physical changes we have observed with the two Alphas in our custody. I believe now, without a doubt, these new infected undead operate on a hive mind basis. The queen controls the workers and the workers protect the queen."

Men in black combat gear burst onto the screen, three shots rapidly flashed and the undead version of her family fell. Quickly and efficiently they laid out body bags and hauled all five of them out of the store.

The video ended and Kelle clicked on the newest file, which was a report. Reading quickly she was amazed by what she learned. Words and phrases flashed in her mind as she read. DNA marker... Predisposed to violence... Virus mutation. Something in her DNA made it possible for her to become what she was.

Snapping back to the present, she laid down on the barn's dirty wooden floor. Curling up like the child she used to be, she didn't so much fall asleep as stop being awake. She had no fear of being killed in her sleep, her children would protect her.

OTHER BOOKS BY J.B. HAVENS

<u>SCI-FI HORROR:</u>

ZOMBIE INSTINCT SERIES

Molly: The Beginning

Molly: Immersion

Molly: Reemergence

ANTHOLOGIES AND SHORT STORIES

Beyond the Night: An Anthology

Ashes & Madness: A Molly Everett Short Story

High Tech/Low Life: An Easytown Novels Anthology

Snap

<u>MILITARY SUSPENSE:</u>

STEEL CORPS SERIES

Core of Steel

Hardened by Steel

Forged by Steel

Bound by Steel

Solid Steel

Steel Corps/Trident Security Crossovers with Samantha
A. Cole

No Way in Hell

Romance:

Antelope Rock Series
co-authored with Samantha A. Cole
Wannabe in Wyoming
Wistful in Wyoming

ABOUT J.B. HAVENS

J.B. Havens lives in rural Pennsylvania, and is a wife and mother of three, a boy and twin girls. She has a love for a good cheesesteak and anything that involves coffee or chocolate. When she's not caring for her family, she is busy researching and writing her next novel.

Find JB on her website where you can find character bios and even a short story or two. She loves to hear from readers, so reach out and tell her what you think!

Connect with J.B.

Facebook
Haven's Haven Facebook Group
Twitter